THE
METROPOLITAN
PROTECTIVES

BY

CHARLES DICKENS

British Library Cataloguing-in-Publication Data
A catalogue record for this book is available from
the British Library

Contents

CHARLES DICKENS

Charles John Huffam Dickens was born in Landport, Portsmouth in 1812. When he was ten years old, his family settled in Camden Town, a poor neighbourhood of London. A defining moment in the young Dickens' life came only two years later, when his father – the inspiration for the character of Mr Micawber in *David Copperfield* – was imprisoned in the Marshalsea debtor's prison. As a result, Dickens was sent to Warren's blacking factory, where he worked in appalling conditions and gained a first-hand acquaintance with poverty. After three years Dickens resumed his education, but the experience was highly formative for him, and would later be fictionalised in both *David Copperfield* and *Great Expectations*.

Dickens' writing career began in around 1830, when he started to write for the journals *The Mirror of Parliament* and *The True Sun*. Three years later, he became parliamentary journalist for *The Morning Chronicle*, and also began to have some successes with his fiction: His first short story, A 'Dinner at Popular Walk', appeared in the *Monthly Magazine* in December of 1833, and his first book, a collection titled *Sketches by Boz*, was published in 1836. However, his real breakthrough came in 1837, with the serialised publication of *Posthumous Papers of the Pickwick Club* – the work was hugely popular, and transformed Dickens into a well-known literary figure.

Over the next few years, at an almost incredible rate, Dickens wrote *Oliver Twist* (1837-39), *Nicholas Nickleby* (1838-39) and *The Old Curiosity Shop* and *Barnaby Rudge* (1840-41). In 1842, he travelled with his wife to the United States and Canada (where he gave lectures denouncing slavery), and in the years following produced his five 'Christmas Books'. During the fifties, after brief spells living in Italy and Switzerland, he continued to write at a seemingly inexhaustible pace, producing some of his best work: David Copperfield (1849-50), Bleak House (1852-53), Hard Times (1854), Little *Dorrit* (1857), *A Tale of Two Cities* (1859), and *Great Expectations* (1861).

During the latter stages of his life, Dickens turned his focus from writing to giving readings. In 1869, during one such reading, he collapsed, showing symptoms of a mild stroke. He died at home one year later, aged 58. He was buried in the Poets' Corner of Westminster Abbey, where the inscription on his tomb reads: "He was a sympathiser to the poor, the suffering, and the oppressed; and by his death, one of England's greatest writers is lost to the world." Dickens is now regarded as the greatest writer of the Victorian era, and one of the greatest English authors since Shakespeare.

The Metropolitan Protectives

Nervous old ladies, dyspeptic half-pay officers, suspicious quidnuncs, plot-dreading diplomatists, and grudging rate-payers, all having the fear of the forthcoming Industrial Invasion before their eyes, are becoming very anxious respecting the adequate efficiency of the London Police. Horrible rumours are finding their way into most of the clubs: reports are permeating into the tea-parties of suburban dowagers which darkly shadow forth dire mischief and confusion, the most insignificant result whereof is to be (of course) the overthrow of the British Constitution. Conspiracies of a comprehensive character are being hatched in certain back parlours, in certain back streets behind Mr Cantelo's Chicken Establishment in Leicester Square. A complicated web of machination is being spun – we have it on the authority of a noble peer – against the integrity of the Austrian Empire, at a small coffee-shop in Soho. Prussia is being menaced by twenty-four determined Poles and Honveds in the attics of a cheap *restaurateur* in the Haymarket. Lots are being cast for the assassination of Louis Napoleon, in the inner parlours of various cigar shops. America, as we learn from that mighty lever of the civilised world, the 'New York Weekly Herald' – at whose nod, it is well known, kings tremble on their thrones, and the earth shakes – is of opinion that the time bids fair for a descent of Red Republicans on Manchester. The English policemen have been tampered with, and are suborned. The great Mr Justice Maule can't find one anywhere. In short, the peace of the entire continent of Europe may be considered as already gone. When the various conspiracies now on foot are ripe, the armies of the disaffected of all nations which are to land at the various British ports under pretence of 'assisting' at the Great Glass show, are to be privately and confidentially drilled in secret *Champs de Mars*, and armed with weapons, stealthily abstracted from the Tower of London: while the Metropolitan Police and the Guards, both horse and foot, will fraternise, and (to a man) pretend to be fast asleep.

Neither have our prudent prophets omitted to foretell minor disasters. Gangs of burglars from the counties of Surrey, Sussex, and Lancashire, are also to fraternise in London, and to 'rifle, rob, and plunder,' as uninterruptedly as if every man's house were a mere Castle of Andalusia. Pickpockets – not in single spies but in whole battalions – are to arrive from Paris and Vienna, and are to fall into compact organisation (through the medium of interpreters) with the united swell-mobs of London, Liverpool, and Manchester!

In short, it would appear that no words can express our fearful condition, so well, as Mr Croaker's in 'The Good Natured Man.' 'I am so frightened,' says he, 'that I scarce know whether I sit, stand, or go. Perhaps at this moment I am treading on lighted matches, blazing brimstone, and barrels of gunpowder. They are preparing to blow me up into the clouds. Murder! We shall be all burnt in our beds!'

Now, to the end that the prophets and their disciples may rest quietly in *their* beds, we have benevolently abandoned our own bed for some three nights or so, in order to report the results of personal inquiry into the condition and system of the Protective Police of the Metropolis: the Detective Police has been already described in the first volume of 'Household Words.' If, after our details of the patience, promptitude, order, vigilance, zeal, and judgment; which watch over the peace of the huge Babylon when she sleeps, the fears of the most apprehensive be not dispelled, we shall have quitted our pillow, and plied our pen in vain! But we have no such distrust.

Although the Metropolitan Police Force consists of nineteen superintendents, one hundred and twenty-four inspectors, five hundred and eighty-five serjeants, and four thousand seven hundred and ninety-seven constables, doing duty at twenty-five stations; yet, so uniform is the order of proceeding in all, and so fairly can the description of what is done at one station be taken as a specimen of what is done at the others, that, without farther preface, we shall take the reader into custody, and convey him at once to the Police Station, in Bow Street, Covent Garden.

A policeman keeping watch and ward at the wicket gives us admission, and we proceed down a long passage into an outer room, where there is a barrack bedstead, on which we observe Police-constable Clark, newly relieved, asleep, and snoring most portentously – a little exhausted, perhaps, by nine hours' constant walking on his beat. In the right-hand corner of this room – which is a bare room like a guard-house without the drums and muskets – is a dock, or space railed off for prisoners: opposite, a window breast-high at which an Inspector always presides day and night to hear charges. Passing by a corner-door into his office on the other side of this window, we find it much like any other office – inky, dull, and quiet – papers stuck against the walls – perfect library of old charges on shelves overhead – stools and desks – a hall-porter's chair, little used – gaslights – fire – sober clock. At one desk stands a policeman, duly coated and caped, looking stiffly over his glazed stock at a handbill he is copying. Two Inspectors sit near, working away at a great rate with noisy pens that sound like little rattles.

The clock points a quarter before nine. One of the Inspectors takes under his arm a slate, the night's muster roll, and an orderly book. He proceeds to the Yard. The gas jet, shining from the office through its window, and a couple of street lamps indistinctly light the place.

On the appearance of the inspecting officer in the yard, and at the sound of the word 'Attention!' about seventy white faces, peering out above half-a-dozen parallel lines of dark figures, fall into military ranks in 'open order.' A man from each section – a Serjeant – comes forward to form the staff of the commanding officer. The roll is called over, and certain men are told off as a Reserve, to remain at the station for any exigencies that may arise. The book is then opened, and the Inspector reads aloud a series of warnings. P. C. John Jones, J, No. 202, was discovered drunk on duty on such a day, and dismissed the force. Serjeant Jenkins did not report that a robbery had been complained of in such a street, and is suspended for a month. The whole division are then enlightened as to the names, addresses, ages, and heights, of all persons who have been 'missing' from a radius of fifteen miles from Charing Cross (the police definition of the Metropolis) since the previous night; as to the colours of their hair, eyes, and clothes; as to the cut of their coats, the fashion and material of their gowns, the shape of their hats or bonnets, the make of their boots. So minute and definite are all these personal descriptions, that a P. C. (the official ellipsis for Police Constable) must be very sleepy, or unusually dull of observation, if, in the event of his meeting with any of these missing individuals, he does not put them in train of restoration to their anxious friends. Lost articles of property are then enumerated and described with equal exactness. When we reflect that the same routine is being performed at the same moment at the head of every police regiment or division in the Metropolis, it seems extraordinary how any thing or person *can* be lost in London. Among the trifles enumerated as 'found,' are a horse and cart, a small dog, a brooch, a baby, and a firkin of butter.

Emotion is no part of a policeman's duty. If felt, it must be suppressed: he listens as stolidly to the following account of the baby, as to the history of the horse and cart, the little dog, the brooch, and the butter.

S. DIVISION. Found, at Eight and a quarter P.M., on the 2nd instant by [a gentleman named], of Bayham Street, Camden Town, on the step of his door, the body of a new-born Infant, tied up in a Holland Bag. Had on a Calico Bed-gown and Muslim Cap, trimmed with Satin Ribbon. Also a Note, stating, 'Any one who finds this precious burthen, pay him the last duties which a Mother – much in distress and trouble of mind – is unable to do. May the blessing of God be on you!'

The book is closed. The mother 'much in distress and trouble of mind,' is shut up with it; and the Inspector proceeds to make his inspection. He marches past each rank. The men, one by one, produce their kit; consisting of lantern, rattle, and staff. He sees that each man is clean and properly provided for the duties of the night. Returning to his former station amidst the serjeants, he gives the word 'Close up!'

The men now form a compact body, and the serjeants take their stand at the head of their respective ranks. But, before this efficient body of troops deploy to their various beats, they are addressed by the superior officer much as a colonel harangues his regiment before going into action. The Inspector's speech – sharp and pithily delivered – is something to this effect:

'Now, men, I must again beg of you to be very careful in your examination of empty houses. See that the doors are fast; and, if not, search for any persons unlawfully concealed therein. Number nineteen section will allow no destitute parties to herd together under the Adelphi arches. Section Number twenty-four will be very particular in insisting on all gentlemen's carriages [it is an opera night] keeping the rank, close to the kerb-stone, and in cautioning the coachmen not to leave their horses. Be sure and look sharp after flower-girls. Offering flowers for sale is a pretence. The girls are either beggars or thieves; but you must exercise great caution. You must not interfere with them unless you actually hear them asking charity, or see them trying pockets, or engaged in actual theft. The chief thing, however, is the empty houses; thieves get from them into the adjoining premises, and then there's a burglary. – 'Tention, to the left face, march!'

The sections march off in Indian file, and the Inspector returns to his office by one door, while the half-dozen 'Reserves' go into the outer-room by another. The former, now buttons on his great coat: and, after supper, will visit every beat in the division, to see that the men are at their duties. The other Inspector remains, to take the charges.

A small man, who gives his name, Mr Spills, (or for whom that name will do in this place as well as another), presents himself at the half-open window to complain of a gentleman now present, who is stricken in years, bald, well dressed, staid in countenance respectable in appearance, and exceedingly drunk. He gazes at his accuser from behind the dock, with lack-lustre penitence, as that gentleman elaborates his grievance to the patient Inspector; who, out of a tangle of digressions and innuendoes dashed with sparkling scraps of club-room oratory, extracts – not without difficulty – the substance of the complaint, and reduces it to a charge of 'drunk and disorderly.' The culprit, it seems, not half an hour ago – purely by accident – found his way into Craven Street, Strand. Though there are upwards of forty doors in Craven street, he *would* kick, and thump, and batter the complainant's door. No other door would do. The complainant don't know why; the delinquent don't know why; nobody knows why. No entreaty, no expostulation, no threat, could induce him to transfer his favours to any other door in the neighbourhood. He was a perfect stranger to Mr Spills; yet, when Mr Spills presented himself at the gate of his castle in answer to the thundering summons, the prisoner insisted on finishing the evening at the domestic supper-table of the Spills family. Finally, the prisoner emphasised his claim on Mr Spills's hospitality by striking Mr Spills on the mouth. This led to his being immediately handed over to the custody of a P. C.

The defendant answers the usual questions as to name and condition, with a drowsy indifference peculiar to the muddled. But, when the Inspector asks his age, a faint ray of his spirit shines through him. What is that to the police? Have they anything to do with the census? They may lock him up, fine him, put him in jail, work him on the tread-mill, if they like. All this is in their power; he knows the law well enough, Sir; but they can't make him tell his age – and he won't – won't do it, Sir! – At length, after having been mildly pressed, and cross-examined, and coaxed, he passes his fingers through the few grey hairs that fringe his bad head, and suddenly roars:

'Well then: Five-and-twenty!'

All the policemen laugh. The prisoner – but now triumphant in his retort – checks himself, endeavours to stand erect, and surveys them with defiance.

'Have you anything about you, you would like us to take care of?' This is the usual apology for searching a drunken prisoner: searches cannot be enforced except in cases of felony.

Before the prisoner can answer, one of the Reserves eases him of his property. Had his adventures been produced in print, they could scarcely have been better described than by the following articles: a pen-knife, an empty sandwich-box, a bunch of keys, a bird's-eye handkerchief, a sovereign, fivepence in half-pence, a tooth-pick, and a pocket-book. From his neck is drawn a watch-guard, cut through, – no watch.

When he is sober, he will be questioned as to his loss; a description of the watch, with its maker's name and number will be extracted from him; it will be sent round to every station; and, by this time to-morrow night, every pawnbroker in the Metropolis will be asked whether such a watch has been offered as a pledge? Most probably it will be recovered and restored before he has time to get tipsy again – and when he has, he will probably lose it again.

'When shall I have to appear before the magistrate?' asks the prosecutor.

'At ten o'clock to-morrow morning,' – and so ends that case.

There is no peace for the Inspector. During the twenty-four hours he is on duty, his window is constantly framing some new picture. For some minutes, a brown face with bright black eyes has been peering impatiently from under a quantity of tangled black hair and a straw hat behind Mr Spills. It now advances to the window.

'Have you got e'er a gipsy woman here, sir?'

'No gipsy woman to-night.'

'Thank'ee, sir:' and the querist retires to repeat this new reading of 'Shepherds, I have lost my love,' at every other station-house, till he finds her – and bails her.

Most of the constables who have been relieved from duty by the nine o'clock men have now dropped in, and are detailing anything worthy of a report to their respective serjeants. The serjeants enter these occurrences on a printed form. Only one is presented, now:

P. C. 67 reports that, at 5$\frac{1}{2}$ P.M., a boy, named Philip Isaac was knocked down, in Bow Street, by a horse belonging to Mr Parks, a Newsvender. He was taken to Charing X Hospital, and sent home, slightly bruised.

The Inspector has not time to file this document before an earnest-looking man comes to the window. Something has happened which evidently causes him more pain than resentment.

'I am afraid we have been robbed. My name is Parker, of the firm of Parker and Tide, Upholsterers. This afternoon at three o'clock, our clerk handed to a young man who is our collector, (he is only nineteen), about ninety-six pounds, to take to the bank. He ought to have been back in about fifteen minutes; but he hadn't come back at six o'clock. I went to the bank to see if the cash had been paid in, and it had *not*.'

'Be good enough to describe his person and dress, sir,' says the Inspector, taking out a printed form called 'a Route.'

These are minutely detailed and recorded. 'Has he any friends or relatives in London?'

The applicant replies by describing the residence and condition of the youth's father and uncle. The Inspector orders 'Ninety-two' (one of the Reserves) to go with the gentleman, 'and see what he can make of it.' The misguided delinquent's chance of escape will be lessened every minute. Not only will his usual haunts be visited in the course of the night by Ninety-two; but his description will be known, before morning, by *every* police officer on duty. This Route, – which is now being copied by a Reserve into a book – will be passed on, presently, to the next station. There, it will again be copied; passed on to the next; copied; forwarded – and so on until it shall have made the circuit of all the Metropolitan stations. In the morning, that description will be read to the men going on duty. 'Long neck, light hair, brown clothes, low crowned hat,' and so on.

A member of the E division throws a paper on the window-sill, touches his hat, exclaims, 'Route, sir!' and departs.

The Routes are coming in all night long. A lady has lost her purse in an omnibus. Here is a description of the supposed thief – a woman who sat next to the lady – and here are the dates and numbers of the bank notes, inscribed on the paper with exactness. On the back, is an entry of the hour at which the paper was received at, and sent away from, every station to which it has yet been. A Reserve is called in to book the memorandum; and in a quarter of an hour he is off with it to the station next on the Route. Not only are these notices read to the men at each relief, but the most important of them are inserted in the *Police Gazette*, the especial literary organ of the Force, which is edited by one of its members.

A well dressed youth about eighteen years of age, now leans over the window to bring himself as near to the Inspector as possible. He whispers in a broad Scotch accent:

'I am destitute. I came up from Scotland to find one Saunders M'Alpine, and I *can't* find him, and I have spent all my money. I have not a farthing left. I want a night's lodging.'

'Reserve!' The Inspector wastes no words in a case like this.

'Sir.'

'Go over to the relieving officer and ask him to give this young man a night in the casual ward.'

The policeman and the half-shamed suppliant go out together.

'That is a genuine tale,' remarks the Inspector.

'Evidently a fortune-seeking young Scotchman,' we venture to con-
jecture, 'who has come to London upon too slight an invitation, and
with too slender a purse. He has an honest face, and won't know want
long. He may die Lord Mayor.'

The Inspector is not sanguine in such cases. 'He *may*,' he says.

There is a great commotion in the outer office. Looking through the
window, we see a stout bustling woman who announces herself as a
complainant, three female witnesses, and two policemen. This solemn
procession moves towards the window; yet we look in vain for a prisoner. The prisoner is in truth invisible on the floor of the dock, so one
of his guards is ordered to mount him on a bench. He is a handsome,
dirty, curly-headed boy about the age of seven, though he says he is
nine. The prosecutrix makes her charge.

'Last Sunday, sir, (if you please, sir, I keep a cigar and stationer's
shop), this here little creetur breaks one of my windows, and the moment after, I loses a box of paints –'

'Value?' asks the Inspector, already entering the charge, after one
sharp look at the child.

'Value, sir? Well, I'll say eight-pence. Well, sir, to-night again, just
before shutting up, I hears another pane go smash. I looks out, and I
sees this same little creetur a running aways. I runs after him, and
hands him over to the police.'

The child does not exhibit the smallest sign of fear or sorrow. He
does not even whimper. He tells his name and address, when asked
them, in a straightforward business-like manner, as if he were quite
used to the whole proceeding. He is locked up; and the prosecutrix is
desired to appear before the Magistrate in the morning to substantiate
her charge.

'A child so young, a professional thief!'

'Ah! These are the most distressing cases we have to deal with. The
number of children brought here, either as prisoners, or as having been
lost, is from five to six thousand per annum. Juvenile crime and its
forerunner – the neglect of children by their parents – is still on the
increase. That's the experience of the whole Force.'

'If some place were provided at which neglected children could be
made to pass their time, instead of in the market and streets – say, in

industrial schools provided by the nation – juvenile delinquency would very much decrease? –'

'I believe, sir, (and I speak the sentiments of many experienced officers in the Force,) that it would be much lessened, and that the expense of such establishments would be saved in a very short time out of the police and county rates. Let alone morality altogether.'

And the Inspector resumes his writing. For a little while we are left to think, to the ticking of the clock.

There are six hundred and fifty-six gentlemen in the English House of Commons assembling in London. There is not one of those gentlemen who may not, in one week, if he choose, acquire as dismal a knowledge of the Hell upon earth in which he lives, in regard of these children, as this Inspector has – as we have – as no man can by possibility shut out, who will walk this town with open eyes observant of what is crying to GOD in the streets. If we were one of those six hundred and fifty-six, and had the courage to declare that we know the day *must come* when these children must be taken, by the strong hand, out of our shameful public ways, and must be rescued – when the State must (no will, or will not, in the case, but must) take up neglected and ignorant children wheresoever they are found, severely punishing the parents when they can be found, too, and forcing them, if they have any means of existence, to contribute something towards the reclamation of their offspring, but never again entrusting them with the duties they have abandoned; – if we were to say this, and were to add that as the day must come, it cannot come too soon, and had best come now – Red Tape would arise against us in ten thousand shapes of virtuous opposition, and cocks would crow, and donkeys would bray, and owls would hoot, and strangers would be espied, and houses would be counted out, and we should be satisfactorily put down. Meanwhile, in Aberdeen, the horror has risen to that height, that against the law, the authorities have by force swept their streets clear of these unchristian objects, and have, to the utmost extent of their illegal power, successfully done this very thing. Do none of the six hundred and fifty-six know of it – do none of them look into it – do none of them lay down their newspapers when they read of a baby sentenced for the third, fourth, fifth, sixth, seventh time to imprisonment and whipping, and ask themselves the question, 'Is there any earthly thing this child can

The discovery of a suicide – an illustration by Henry Aneley

do when this new sentence is fulfilled, but steal again, and be again imprisoned and again flogged, until, a precocious human devil, it is shipped away to corrupt a new world?' Do none of the six hundred and fifty-six, care to walk from Charing Cross to Whitechapel – to look into Wentworth Street – to stray into the lanes of Westminster – to go into a prison almost within the shadow of their own Victoria Tower – to see with their eyes and hear with their ears, what such childhood is, and what escape it has from being what it is? Well! Red Tape is easier, and tells for more in blue books, and will give you a committee five years long if you like, to enquire whether the wind ever blows, or the rain ever falls – and then you can talk about it, and do nothing.

Our meditations are suddenly interrupted.

'Here's a pretty business!' cries a pale man in a breathless hurry, at the window. 'Somebody has been tampering with my door-lock!'

'How do you mean, sir?'

'Why, I live round the corner, and I had been to the Play, and I left my door on the lock (it's a Chubb!) and I come back, and the lock won't act. It has been tampered with. There either are, or have been, thieves in the place!'

'Reserve!'

'Sir!'

'Take another man with you, and a couple of ladders, and see to this gentleman's house.'

A sallow anxious little man rushes in.

'O! you haven't seen anything of such a thing as a black and tan spaniel, have you?'

'Is it a spaniel dog we have got in the yard?' the Inspector inquires of the jailer.

'No, sir, it's a brown tarrier?'

'O! It can't be my dog then. A brown tarrier? O! Good night, gentlemen! Thank you.'

'Good night, sir.'

The Reserve just now dispatched with the other man and the two ladders, returns, gruff-voiced and a little disgusted.

'Well? what's up round the corner?'

'Nothing the matter with the lock, sir. I opened it with the key directly!'

We fall into a doze before the fire. Only one little rattle of a pen is springing now, for the other Inspector has put on his great-coat and gone out, to make the round of his beat and look after his men. We become aware in our sleep of a scuffling on the pavement outside. It approaches, and becomes noisy and hollow on the boarded floor within. We again repair to the window.

A very ill-looking woman in the dock. A very stupid little gentleman, very much overcome with liquor, and with his head extremely towzled, endeavouring to make out the meaning of two immoveable Policemen, and indistinctly muttering a desire to know 'war it's awr abow.'

'Well?' says the Inspector, possessed of the case in a look.

'I was on duty, sir, in Lincoln's Inn Fields just now,' says one of the Policemen, 'when I see this gent' –

Here, 'this gent,' with an air of great dignity, again observers, 'Mirrer Insperrer, I requesherknow war it's awr ABOW.'

'We'll hear you presently, sir. Go on!'

– 'when I see this gent, in conversation against the railings with this woman. I requested him to move on, and observed his watch-guard hanging loose out of his pocket. "You've lost your watch," I said. Then I turned to her! "And you've got it," I said. "I an't," she said. Then she said, turning to him, "You know you've been in company with many others to-night, flower-girls, and a lot more." "I shall take *you*," I said, anyhow. Then I turned my lantern on her, and saw this silver watch, with the glass broke, lying behind her on the stones. Then I took her into custody, and the other constable brought the gent along.'

'Jailer!' says the Inspector.

'Sir!'

'Keep your eye on her. Take care she don't make away with anything – and send for Mrs Green.'

The accused sits in a corner of the dock, quite composed, with her arms under her dirty shawl, and says nothing. The Inspector folds a charge-sheet, and dips his pen in the ink.

'Now, sir, your name, if you please?'

'Ba – a.'

'*That* can't be your name, sir. What name does he say, Constable?' The second Constable 'seriously inclines his ear;' the gent being a short man, and the second constable a tall one. 'He says his name's Bat, sir.' (Getting at it after a good deal of trouble.)

'Where do you live, Mr Bat?'

'Lamber.'

'And what are you? – what business are you, Mr Bat?'

'Fesher,' says Mr Bat, again collecting dignity.

'Profession, is it? Very good, sir. What's your profession?'

'Solirrer,' returns Mr Bat.

'Solicitor, of Lambeth. Have you lost anything besides your watch sir?'

'I am nor aware – lost – any – arrickle – prorrery,' says Mr Bat.

The Inspector has been looking at the watch.

'What do you value this watch at, sir?'

'Ten pound,' says Mr Bat, with unexpected promptitude.

'Hardly worth so much as that, I should think?'

'Five pound five,' says Mr Bat. 'I doro how much. I'm not par-TICK-ler,' this word costs Mr Bat a tremendous effort, 'abow the war. It's not my war. It's a frez of my.'

'If it belongs to a friend of yours, you wouldn't like to lose it, I suppose?'

'I doro,' says Mr Bat, 'I'm nor any ways par-TICK-ler abow the war. It's a frez of my;' which he afterwards repeats at intervals, scores of times. Always as an entirely novel idea.

Inspector writes. Brings charge-sheet to window. Reads same to Mr Bat.

'You charge this woman, sir,' – her name, age, and address have been previously taken – 'with robbing you of your watch. I won't trouble you to sign the sheet, as you are not in good writing order. You'll have to be here this morning – it's now two – at a quarter before ten.'

'Never get up 'till har par,' says Mr Bat, with decision.

'You'll have to be here this morning,' repeats the Inspector placidly, 'at a quarter before ten. If you don't come, we shall have to send for you, and that might be unpleasant. Stay a bit. Now, look here. I have written it down. "Mr Bat to be in Bow Street, quarter before ten." Or I'll even say to make it easier to you, a quarter past. There! "Quarter past ten." Now, let me fold this up and put it in your pocket; and when your landlady, or whoever it is at home, finds it there, she'll take care to call you.'

All of which is elaborately done for Mr Bat. A constable who has skilfully taken a writ out of the unconscious Mr Bat's pocket in the meantime, and has discovered from the indorsement that he has given his name and address correctly, receives instructions to put Mr Bat into a cab and send him home.

'And, Constable,' says the Inspector to the first man, musing over the watch as he speaks, 'do you go back to Lincoln's Inn Fields, and look about, and you'll find, somewhere, the little silver pin belonging to the handle. She has done it in the usual way, and twisted the pin right out.'

'What mawrer is it?' says Mr Bat, staggering back again, 'T'morrow-mawrer?'

'Not to-morrow morning. This morning.'

'*This* mawrer?' says Mr Bat. 'How can it be this mawrer? *War* is this aur abow?'

As there is no present probability of his discovering 'what it is all about,' he is conveyed to his cab; and a very indignant matron with a very livid face, a trembling lip, and a violently heaving breast, presents herself.

'Which I wishes to complain immediate on Pleeseman forty-two and fifty-three and insistes on the charge being took; and that I will substantiate before the magistrates to-morrow morning, and what is more will prove and which is saying a great deal sir!'

'You needn't be in a passion, you know, here, ma'am. Everything will be done correct.'

'Which I *am* not in a passion sir and everythink shalt be done correct, if you please!' drawing herself up with a look designed to freeze the whole division. 'I make a charge immediate,' very rapidly, 'against pleesemen forty-two and fifty-three, and insistes on the charge being took.'

'I can't take it till I know what it is,' returns the patient Inspector, leaning on the window-sill, and making no hopeless effort, as yet, to write it down. 'How was it, ma'am?'

'This is how it were, sir. I were standing at the door of my own 'ouse.'

'Where is your house, ma'am?'

'*Where* is my house, sir?' with the freezing look.

'Yes, ma'am. Is it in the Strand, for instance.'

'No, sir,' with indignant triumph. 'It is *not* in the Strand!'

'Where then, ma'am?'

'Where then, sir?' with severe sarcasm.

'I *ope* it is in Doory Lane.'

'In Drury Lane. And what is your name, ma'am?'

'*My* name, sir?' with inconceivable scorn. 'My name is Megby.'

'Mrs Megby?'

'Sir, I *ope* so!' with the previous sarcasm. Then, very rapidly, 'I keep a Coffee house, as I will substantiate to-morrow morning and what is more will prove and that is saying a great deal.' Then, still more rapidly, 'I wish to make a charge immediate against pleesemen forty-two and fifty-three!'

'Well, ma'am, be so good as make it.'

'I were standing at my door,' falling of a sudden into a genteel and impressive slowness, 'in conversation with a friend, a gentleman from the country which his name is Henery Lupvitch, *Es*-quire –'

'Is he here, ma'am?'

'No, sir,' with surpassing scorn. 'He is *not* here!'

'Well, ma'am?'

'With Henery Lupvitch *Es*-quire, and which I had just been hissuing directions to two of my servants, when here come between us a couple of female persons which I know to be the commonest dirt, and pushed against me.'

'Both of them pushed against you?'

'No sir,' with scorn and triumph, 'they did *not*! *One* of 'em pushed against me' – A dead stoppage, expressive of implacable gentility.

'Well, ma'am – did you say anything then?'

'I ask your parding. Did I which, sir?' As compelling herself to fortitude under great provocation.

'Did you say anything?'

'I *ope* I did. I says, how dare you do that ma'am?'

Stoppage again. Expressive of a severe desire that those words be instantly taken down.

'You said how dare you do that?'

' "Nobody," continuing to quote with a lofty and abstracted effort of memory, "never interfered with you." She replies, "That's nothink to you, ma'am. Never you mind." '

Another pause, expressive of the same desire as before. Much incensed at nothing resulting.

The Metropolitan Protectives

'She then turns back between me and Henery Lupvitch *Es*-quire, and commits an assault upon me, which I am not a acquisition and will not endoor or what is more submit to.'

What Mrs Megby means by the particular expression that she is not an acquisition, does not appear; but she turns more livid, and not only her lip but her whole frame trembles as she solemnly repeats, 'I am not a acquisition.'

'Well, ma'am. Then forty-two and fifty-three came up –'

'No they did *not*, sir; nothink of the sort! – I called 'em up.'

'And you said?'

'Sir?' with tremendous calmness.

'You said?' –

'*I made the obserwation*,' with strong emphasis and exactness, 'I give this person in charge for assaulting of me. Forty-two says, 'O you're not hurt. Don't make a disturbance here. Fifty-three likewys declines to take the charge. Which,' with greater rapidity than ever, 'is the two pleesemen I am here to appear against; and will be here at nine to-morrow morning, or at height if needful, or at sivin – hany hour – and as a ouseholder demanding the present charge to be regularly hentered against pleesemen respectually numbered forty-two and fifty-three, which shall be substantiated by day or night or morning – which is more – for I am not a acquisition, and what those pleesemen done sir they shall answer!'

The Inspector – whose patience is not in the least affected – being now possessed of the charge, reduces it to a formal accusation against two P. C's., for neglect of duty, and gravely records it in Mrs Megby's own words – with such fidelity that, at the end of every sentence when it is read over, Mrs Megby, comparatively softened, repeats, 'Yes, sir, which it is correct!' and afterwards signs, as if her name were not half long enough for her great revenge.

On the removal of Mrs Megby's person, Mr Bat, to our great amazement, is revealed behind her.

'I say! Is it t'morrow mawrer?' asks Mr Bat in confidence.

'He has got out of the cab,' says the Inspector, whom nothing surprises, 'and will be brought in, in custody, presently! No. This morning. Why don't you go home?'

'*This* mawrer!' says Mr Bat, profoundly reflecting. 'How car it be *this* mawrer. It must be yesserday mawrer.'

'You had better make the best of your way home, sir,' says the Inspector.

'No offence is interrer,' says Mr Bat. 'I happened to be passing – this dirrertion – when – saw door open – kaymin. It's a frez of my – I am nor –' he is quite unequal to the word particular now, so concludes with 'you no war I me! – I am aw ri! I shall be here in the mawrer!' and stumbles out again.

The watch stealer, who has been removed, is now brought back. Mrs Green (the searcher) reports to have found upon her some halfpence, two pawnbroker's duplicates, and a comb. All produced.

'Very good. You can lock her up now, jailer. – What does she say?'

'She says can she have her comb, sir?'

'Oh yes. She can have her comb. Take it!' And away she goes to the cells, a dirty unwholesome object, designing, no doubt, to comb herself out for the magisterial presence in the morning.

'O! Please sir, you have got two French ladies here, in brown shot silk?' says a woman with a basket. (We have changed the scene to the Vine Street Station House, but its general arrangement is just the same.)

'Yes.'

'Will you send 'em in, this fowl and bread for supper, please?'

'They shall have it. Hand it in.'

'Thank'ee, sir. Good night, sir!'

The Inspector has eyed the woman, and now eyes the fowl. He turns it up, opens it neatly with his knife, takes out a little bottle of brandy artfully concealed within it, puts the brandy on a shelf as confiscated, and sends in the rest of the supper.

What is this very neat new trunk in a corner, carefully corded?

It is here on a charge of 'drunk and incapable.' It was found in Piccadilly to-night (with a young woman sitting on it) and is full of good clothes, evidently belonging to a domestic servant. Those clothes will be rags soon, and the drunken woman will die of gin, or be drowned in the river.

We are dozing by the fire again, and it is past three o'clock when the stillness (only invaded at intervals by the head voices of the two French ladies talking in their cell – no other prisoners seem to be awake,) is broken by the complaints of a woman and the cries of a child. The outer door opens noisily, and the complaints and the cries come nearer, and come into the dock.

'What's this?' says the Inspector, putting up the window. 'Don't cry there, don't cry!'

A rough-headed miserable little boy of four or five years old stops in his crying and looks frightened.

'This woman,' says a wet constable, glistening in the gaslight, 'has been making a disturbance in the street for hours, on and off. She says she wants relief. I have warned her off my beat over and over again, sir; but it's of no use. She took at last to rousing the whole neighbourhood.'

'You hear what the constable says. What did you do that for?'

'Because I want relief, sir.'

'If you want relief, why don't you go to the relieving-officer?'

'I've been, sir, God knows; but I couldn't get any. I haven't been under a blessed roof for three nights; but have been prowling the streets the whole night long, sir. And I can't do it any more, sir. And my husband has been dead these eight months, sir. And I've nobody to help me to a shelter or a bit of bread, God knows!'

'You haven't been drinking, have you?'

'Drinking, sir? Me, sir?'

'I am afraid you have. Is that your own child?'

'O yes, sir, he's my child!'

'*He* hasn't been with you in the streets three nights, has he?'

'No, sir. A friend took him in for me, sir; but couldn't afford to keep him any longer, sir, and turned him on my hands this afternoon, sir.'

'You didn't fetch him away yourself, to have him to beg with, I suppose?'

'O no, sir! Heavens knows I didn't, sir!'

'Well!' writing on a slip of paper, 'I shall send the child to the workhouse until the morning, and keep you here. And then, if your story is true, you can tell it to the magistrate, and it will be inquired into.'

'Very well, sir. And God knows I'll be thankful to have it inquired into!'

'Reserve!'

'Sir!'

'Take this child to the workhouse. Here's the order. You go along with this man, my little fellow, and they'll put you in a nice warm bed, and give you some breakfast in the morning. There's a good boy!'

The wretched urchin parts from his mother without a look, and trots contentedly away with the constable. There would be no very strong ties to break here if the constable were taking him to an industrial school. Our honourable friend the member for Red Tape voted for breaking stronger ties than these in workhouses once upon a time. And we seem faintly to remember that he glorified himself upon that measure very much!

We shift the scene to Southwark. It is much the same. We return to Bow Street. Still the same. Excellent method, carefully administered, vigilant in all respects except this main one: prevention of ignorance, remedy for unnatural neglect of children, punishment of wicked parents, interposition of the State, as a measure of human policy, if not of human pity and accountability, at the very source of crime.

Our Inspectors hold that drunkenness as a cause of crime, is in the ratio of two to one greater than any other cause. We doubt if they make due allowance for the cases in which it is the consequence or companion of crime, and not the cause; but, we do not doubt its extensive influence as a cause alone. Of the seven thousand and eighteen charges entered in the books of Bow Street station during 1850, at least half are against persons of both sexes, for being 'drunk and incapable.' If offences be included which have been indirectly instigated by intoxication the proportion rises to at least seventy-five per cent. As a proof of this, it can be demonstrated from the books at head quarters (Scotland Yard) that there was a great and sudden diminution of charges after the wise measure of shutting up public houses at twelve o'clock on Saturday nights.

Towards five o'clock, the number of cases falls off, and the business of the station dwindles down to charges against a few drunken women. We have seen enough, and we retire.

We have not wearied the reader, whom we now discharge, with more than a small part of our experience; we have not related how the two respectable tradesmen, 'happening' to get drunk at 'the House they used,' first fought with one another, then 'dropped into' a policeman; as that witness related in evidence, until admonished by his Inspector concerning the Queen's English: nor how one young person resident near Covent Garden, reproached another young person in a loud tone of voice at three o'clock in the morning, with being 'a shilling minx' – nor how that young person retorted that, allowing herself for the sake of argument to be a minx, she must yet prefer a claim to be a pound minx rather than a shilling one, and so they fell to fighting and were taken into custody – nor how the first minx, piteously declaring that she had 'left her place without a bit of key,' was consoled, before having the police-key turned upon herself, by the dispatch of a trusty constable to secure her goods and chattels from pillage: nor how the two smiths taken up for 'larking' on an extensive scale, were sorely solicitous about 'a centre-punch' which one of them had in his pocket; and which, on being searched (according to custom) for knives, they expected never to see more: nor how the drunken gentleman of independent property – who being too drunk to be allowed to buy a railway ticket, and being most properly refused, most improperly 'dropped into' the Railway authorities – complained to us, visiting his cell, that he was locked up on a foul charge at which humanity revolted, and was not allowed to send for bail, and was *this* the Bill of Rights? We have seen that an incessant system of communication, day and night, is kept up between every station of the force; we have seen, not only crime speedily detected, but distress quickly relieved; we have seen regard paid to every application, whether it be an enquiry after a gipsy woman, or a black-and-tan spaniel, or a frivolous complaint against a constable; we have seen that everything that occurs is written down, to be forwarded to head quarters; we have seen an extraordinary degree of patience habitually exercised in listening to prolix details, in relieving the kernel of a case from its almost impenetrable husk; we have seen how impossible it is for anything of a serious, of even an unusual, nature to happen without being reported; and that if reported, additional force can be immediately supplied from each station; where from twenty to thirty men are always collected while off duty. We have seen that the whole system is well, intelligently, zealously worked; and we have seen, finally, that the addition of a few extra men will be all-sufficient for any exigencies which may arise from the coming influx of visitors.

Believe us, nervous old lady, dyspeptic half-pay, suspicious quidnunc, plot-dreading diplomatist, you may sleep in peace! As for you, trembling rate-payer, it is not to be doubted that, after what you have read, you will continue to pay your eightpence in the pound without a grudge. And if, either you nervous old lady, or you dyspeptic half-pay, or you suspicious quidnunc, or you plot-dreading diplomatist, or you ungrudging rate-payer, have ever seen or heard, or read of, a vast city which a solitary watcher might traverse in the dead of night as he may traverse London, you are far wiser than we. It is daybreak on this third morning of our vigil – on, it may be, the three thousandth morning of our seeing the pale dawn in these hushed and solemn streets. Sleep in peace! If you have children in your house, wake to think of, and to act for, the doomed childhood that encircles you out of doors, from the rising up of the sun unto the going down of the stars, and sleep in greater peace. There is matter enough for real dread there. It is a higher cause than the cause of any rotten government on the Continent of Europe, that, trembling, hears the Marseillaise in every whisper, and dreads a barricade in every gathering of men!

www.ingramcontent.com/pod-product-compliance
Lightning Source LLC
Chambersburg PA
CBHW030544180626
46810CB00005B/1996